S0-AFC-264

J BOWSER
Bowser, Ken,
The conundrum of the crooked crayon /

The Conundrum of the

Crooked Crayon

Written & Illustrated
by Ken Bowser

Solving Mysteries Through
Science, Technology, Engineering, Art & Math

RED
CHAIR
•PRESS•

Egremont, Massachusetts

The Jesse Steam Mysteries are produced and published by:
Red Chair Press LLC   PO Box 333   South Egremont, MA 01258-0333
www.redchairpress.com

 FREE Educator Guide at www.redchairpress.com/free-resources

For My Grandson, Liam

Publisher's Cataloging-In-Publication Data
Names: Bowser, Ken, author, illustrator.
Title: The conundrum of the crooked crayon / written & illustrated by Ken Bowser.

Description: South Egremont, MA : Red Chair Press, [2020] | Series: A
   Jesse Steam mystery | "Solving Mysteries Through Science, Technology,
   Engineering, Art & Math." | Includes a makerspace activity for hands-on
   learning about the strength and angle of the sun's rays. | Summary:
   "While doing spring cleaning in her room, Jesse comes across a crayon
   on her window sill that is curiously bent over. She recalls that the
   crayon was there all winter and not bent at all. Jesse begins to wonder
   what caused the crayon to bend. Using science skills, Jesse discovers
   how the Sun is closest to Earth in summer and that's why the crayon
   melted"--Provided by publisher.

Identifiers: ISBN 9781634409339 (library hardcover) | ISBN 9781634409346
   (paperback) | ISBN 9781634409353 (ebook)

Subjects: LCSH: Crayons--Juvenile fiction. | Ultraviolet radiation--
   Juvenile fiction. | Sunshine--Juvenile fiction. | Seasons--Juvenile
   fiction. | CYAC: Crayons--Fiction. | Sunshine--Fiction. | Seasons--
   Fiction. | LCGFT: Detective and mystery fiction.

Classification: LCC PZ7.B697 Co 2020 (print) | LCC PZ7.B697 (ebook) | DDC
   [Fic]--dc23

LC record available at https://lccn.loc.gov/2019936017

The publisher is not responsible for websites (or their content) that are not
owned by the publisher.

Printed in the United States of America

0520 1P CGF20

Table of Contents

Cast of Characters

Jesse Steam

Amateur sleuth and all-around neat kid. Jesse loves riding her bike, solving mysteries, and most of all, Mr. Stubbs. Jesse is never without her messenger bag and the cool stuff it holds.

Mr. Stubbs

A cat with an attitude, he's the coolest tabby cat in Deanville. Stubbs was a stray cat who strayed right into Jesse's heart. Can you figure out how he got his name?

Professor Peach

A retired university professor. Professor Peach knows tons of cool stuff and is somewhat of a legend in Deanville. He has college degrees in Science, Technology, Engineering, Art and Math.

Emmett

Professor Peach's ever-present pet, white lab rat. He loves cheese balls, and wherever you find The Professor, you're sure to find Emmett—even though he might be difficult to spot!

Clark & Lewis

Jesse's next-door neighbor and sometimes formidable adversary, Clark Johnson, and his slippery, slimy, gross-looking pet frog, Lewis. Yuck.

Dorky Dougy

Clark Johnson's three-year-old, tag-along baby brother. Dougy is never without his stuffed alligator, a rubber knife, and something really goofy to say, like "eleventy-seven."

Kimmy Kat Black

Holder of the Deanville Elementary School Long Jump Record, know-it-all, and self-proclaimed future member of Mensa. Kimmy Kat Black lives near the Spooky Tree.

Liam LePoole

A black belt in karate, and also the captain of the Deanville Community Swimming Pool Cannonball Team. Liam's best friend is Chompy Dog, his stinky, gassy, and frenzied brown Puggle.

Chompy Dog

Liam LePoole's very best friend. Chompy Dog is Liam's stinky, gassy, and frenzied, brown Puggle puppy. His toots and his breath can clear a room in 6.2 seconds.

Miss Teal

The town of Deanville's resident hippy. Miss Teal is the ice cream truck proprietor and purveyor of frozen concoctions of all shapes and sizes.

The Town of Deanville

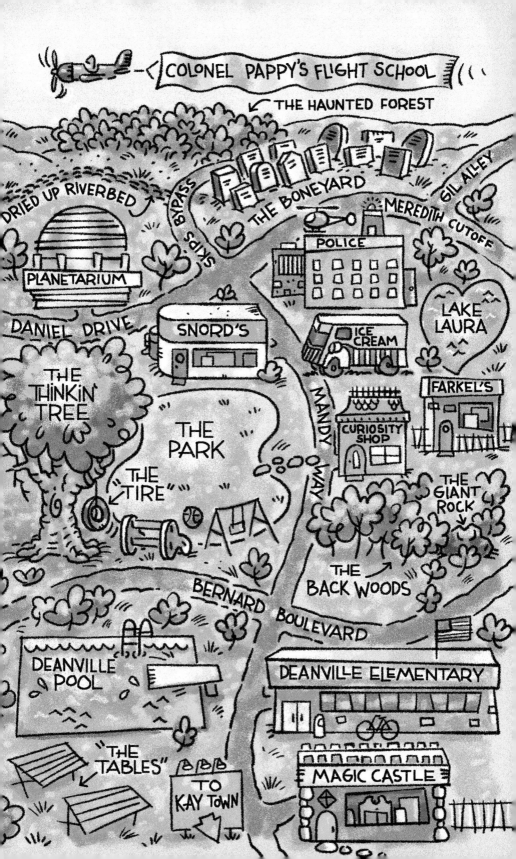

Sunshine on My Shoulders Makes Me Happy

Chapter 1

"Mr. Stubbs! Where are you? You silly cat!" Jesse Steam called out. "It's time for your lunch!" *Where in the world can he be?* Jesse wondered to herself.

"Stuuuub-beeeee. Where *arrrrrrre* you?" she called out in a sing-song voice. She looked under her bed. "Not under there," she mumbled. "Hmmm. Where is that rascal?"

Jesse looked in the cubbyhole beneath the stairs where Stubbs often curled up when he was chilly. *Nope,* she said to herself. *Not there.* She turned and looked in the living room and checked beside the couch.

"Well, there you are!" She laughed. "I should have known to look here from the very beginning. Wherever you find a warm sunbeam, you're sure to find Mr. Stubbs snoozin' away." She chuckled to herself.

"C'mon, Stubby, old boy," Jesse said to the sleeping feline. "We have lots of stuff to do today before we meet the rest of the gang at The Thinkin' Tree. We'll start with organizing my room, and then we can hop on the bike and head to the park."

Jesse and Stubbs headed upstairs to her room, where she had set out the contents of her messenger bag. "I don't think we'll need all of this stuff today," Jesse said to Stubbs, "but it's good to be prepared anyway."

Jesse never went anywhere without her "tools," as she called them. "Ya never know what you're going to need to help solve a mystery," she would often say.

"Journal. Check," she said as she placed it into her bag. "Pen, pencil, and wristwatch, check." In the bag they went. "I'll bring my rubber nose and glasses too. One never knows when they might need an instant disguise." She laughed. "Right, Stubbs?"

Jesse resumed sorting through her bag.
"Calculator, check. I'll bring that. Money.
Check. Better throw some change in there
just in case we see Miss Teal's ice cream
truck," she continued. "Library card. Check."

Jesse took her magnifying glass from her messenger bag. "Hmm. I always bring this. But ya know what? I think I'll leave it here for once," she said to Stubbs as he looked on.

Jesse put the spyglass in its stand on the windowsill. "Let's go, dude!" she said as they headed out for the day.

Look Out! Dougy's Gonna Barf!

Chapter 2

Outside a warm wind blew, and the sun began to peek through the trees as it rose slowly over the neighborhood rooftops. Lengthy shadows stretched out over the driveway like giant fingers, while a mockingbird, perched high on a branch, cast a peculiar-looking silhouette on the lawn.

"What a beautiful summer morning this is," Jesse said to Stubbs as she plopped him into the basket on the front of her bike, his paws hanging over the edge.

"There's not a cloud in the sky," she said to her silly cat. "The weatherman said that this was going to be a scorcher, whatever that means. Something about it being the longest day of the year."

"Hey, do you know what the summer solstice is?" she asked Stubbs. "Me neither."

Riding her bike in the early morning sun, Jesse marveled at the long shadows that she and Stubbs threw across the grass as she pedaled through the park.

"Hey, look at us!" She laughed to Stubbs as she gazed at the distorted shape their shadows created. Jesse waved her hand high up over her head as she pedaled.

"My arm looks like it's a hundred feet long in this wacky shadow." She giggled to Stubbs. "And look at the shape of our wheels! They're not round at all. They're shaped more like eggs than bicycle tires." She laughed out loud.

Jesse and Mr. Stubbs continued their ride through the park, ready to meet up with the rest of the neighborhood kids. With each and every turn their shadow changed.

"Hey, look, Stubby! Now our shadow is right in front of us," she pointed out to Stubbs as they gradually changed direction.

Up ahead, Jesse could see the gang already gathering in the park in the shade under The Thinkin' Tree.

"Hey, guys!" she yelled as she pedaled up and hopped off of her bike. "Hang here for a

minute," she said to Stubbs as she grabbed
her messenger bag.

Clark Johnson was there with his slimy
pet frog Lewis, of course. "Glub gluurp," the

gross frog croaked from Clark's top pocket as Jesse walked up.

"Clark, why must you constantly bring that repulsive critter with you everywhere you go?" Kimmy Kat Black said in her usual condescending way. "As a future member of Mensa, I insist that you keep that disgusting, tailless amphibian elsewhere," she snipped in her snippiest of snippy voices.

"Yeah! It's a sta-gustin tailed fam-ib-ium!" Clark's dorky little brother said back.

"Not a word, Dougy!" They all laughed.

The group played in the cool shade of The Thinkin' Tree for the rest of the morning. The sun grew higher in the sky, and soon

their shadows were no longer stretched out but small and directly under their feet.

"Hey, look at my shadow now!" Jesse held her arms straight out from her sides. "I look like an airplane propeller."

"Me too," Dorky Dougy said, and he began to spin around and around, as fast as he could, with his arms straight out and making airplane sounds with his mouth. "Brrrrt. Brrrrt, brrrrt," he blurted as he spun around, and around, and around.

"I don't feel so good," Dougy said as he stopped spinning and held his stomach. His face turned a funny color.

"Look out, everyone! Dougy's gonna barf!" They all laughed.

I Scream, You Scream. You Know the Rest.

Chapter 3

DING, LING, A-LING, LING, LING!

Just as Dorky Dougy was beginning to turn forty gnarly shades of green and about to puke his guts out from spinning around and around so fast, the kids heard a delightful, wonderful, familiar sound.

DING, LING-A, LING, LING, LING! The sound rang out for a second time.

DING, LING-A, LING, LING, LING! A third.

Silence fell over the group. Their eyes widened as they looked at one another.

"ICE CREAM TRUCK!" Jesse was the first to scream out.

Then, **"ICE CREAM TRUCK!"** The rest of the kids screamed out together with laughter.

"Ice cream?" Dougy said in a puny voice. "I don't feel like ice cream so much, guys."

Miss Teal's ice cream truck came to a stop with its bell still ringing. *DING, LING, A-LING, LING, LING!* It rang out a last time.

"It's a good thing I packed some change in my messenger bag this morning." Jesse

winked at Mr. Stubbs, who was licking his chops at the thought of ice cream.

"I'm gettin' a cherry popsicle," Liam LePoole said as the group crowded around the truck's big window. "I'll share it with Chompy Dog," he said to the other kids.

"Gross! Dog germs! Blech!" They all laughed.

"I believe I shall partake in a Rocket Pop," Kimmy Kat Black said in her smartest voice. "After all, it's only logical that a future astronaut would consume such an appropriate frozen confection," she bragged.

The other kids looked at Kimmy as if she had worms coming out of her ears.

"I still don't feel so good, guys," Dougy said in a wimpy voice.

"One chocolate ice cream cone, please," Jesse said as it was her turn at the window.

Jesse joined the other kids in the park. By now the sun was high up in the June sky and beating down on their heads like laser beams as they sat on the bench with their frozen treats.

"GROSSSSSSS!" Jesse turned just in time to see the kids pointing and laughing hysterically.

Liam's cherry popsicle had slid off of its stick, and it was now melting on the hot

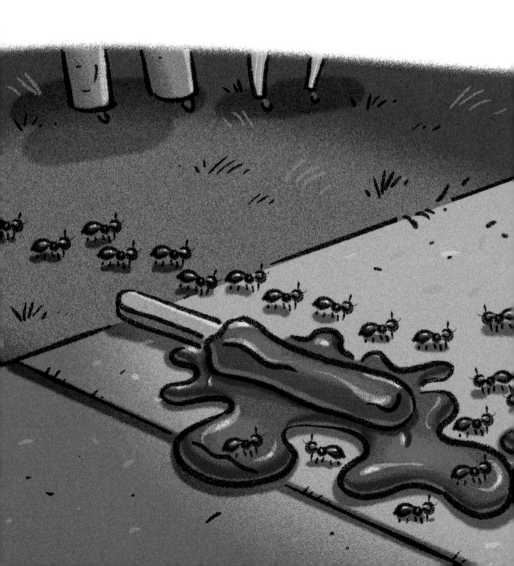

sidewalk—*totally* covered with sticky, crawling ants.

"Chompy Dog! Don't eat that, you deranged mutt!" he said as the crazed dog lapped up the sticky red puddle, ants and all.

Clark's cone was the next to meet its melty fate. The vanilla cone he was enjoying

had become a thawed mess and was running down his forearm, all the way to his elbow.

Then suddenly, the blobby top of Clark's melting treat toppled from its cone and landed right on the top of Dorky Dougy's head with a sloppy plop.

"Dougy's wearing an ice cream hat!" The kids laughed.

One by one, all of the frozen treats fell victim to the blistering summer sun.

"It appears as though my rocket pop has burned up on reentry," Kimmy Kat Black said with a sigh, as her pop fell and dripped its last drop onto the hot sidewalk.

Here Comes the Sun

Chapter 4

"Meow."

Mr. Stubbs curled up in the crook of Jesse's arm as the group lounged on the grass in the park after the ice cream and popsicle debacle. The afternoon sun grew higher in the sky, and the kids' shadows began to grow long again.

"Have you ever wondered just how far away the sun is?" Jesse asked the group as she squinted up into the sky.

"We've gotta be at least a thousand miles from the sun," Clark Johnson said in his boldest voice.

"No way, Clark," Liam LePoole returned. "It's gotta be way further than that."

"Eleventy-forty," Dougy butted in.

"Eleventy-forty what, Dougy?" Liam asked.

"Eleventy-forty miles! That's how far we are from the sun," Dougy shot back.

"NOT A NUMBER, DOUGY!"

"150 million kilometers," Kimmy Kat Black quickly butted in, as only Kimmy Kat Black could. "Based upon my recent book report—which received an A+, by the way—and my vast knowledge on the subject, I can attest to this with some degree of authority." Kimmy was always attesting to something with "some degree of authority." "We orbit the Sun at a distance of approximately 150 million kilometers. This number is actually an average, since we follow an elliptical path. At its closest point, the Earth gets to 149 million kilometers, and at its most distant point, it's 153 million kilometers."

The kids all looked at Kimmy like she had worms coming out of her ears again.

"You're full of bologna, Kimmy," Clark said.

"Yeah! You're full of malooney, Kimmy!" Dougy said.

"What's a kilometer, anyway?" Jesse asked.

"Ah, silly girl," Kimmy snarked back. "A kilometer is a metric unit of measurement equal to 1,000 meters, or about 0.621371 miles. So in layman's terms—the layman being YOU, Jesse—the sun is roughly 92.96 million miles from the earth," Kimmy said in her snarkiest of snarky voices. Kimmy was really good at being snarky, especially when she was right. And it seemed like she was always right. Or at least she *thought* she was.

"Wow. That's a lot of miles," Jesse replied.

Ducks and Rockets and Farting Bananas

Chapter 5

The group hung around the park for another hour or so. They spent a good bit of time looking up at the sky and trying to find shapes in the clouds, along with debating Kimmy's theory on the distance between the Earth and the Sun.

"I see a cloud that looks like a gigantic two-headed duck." Liam chuckled.

"Hey, look. That cloud is shaped just like a rocket with smoke coming out of the back," Kimmy Kat Black said.

"It looks more like a farting banana to me, Kimmy!" Clark joked. All of the kids laughed looking up at the sky.

"Grow up, Clark!" Kimmy snapped at him.

"Well, that's what it looks like to me," Clark snapped right back at her. "You see a rocket. I see a farting banana. What of it?"

"Well, you *would* see something like that, Clark," Kimmy berated. "You and your dumb old frog."

"Well, I think I've had about as much of this fun as I can tolerate for one day," Jesse said as she stood up. "C'mon, Stubby, old boy. Let's make like a banana and split."

"We need to be back home before sunset, and the sun's getting pretty low as it is," Jesse said to the other kids as she waved goodbye.

Jesse and Stubbs loaded back onto her bike and began the short ride home.

As Jesse pedaled, she watched their shadows, just as she did on their morning ride.

"Hey, Stubbs," Jesse called to him in his basket. "Our shadows are just like they were this morning, except now they're going in the other direction." She pointed it out to him. "Did you notice that?" They turned the corner at Snord's Service Station and passed the Deanville Science

Center and Planetarium with its large, shiny, aluminum-domed observatory on top.

"I've always wondered about what that big, round thing on top of the Science Center is." She motioned to Mr. Stubbs. "What do you suppose it is?" Stubbs was already sound asleep in the basket on the front of Jesse's handlebars. "And what's a planetarium anyway?" she asked herself.

As Jesse rode by, she noticed a large banner hanging on the side of the building. The sign read:

"Summer Solstice Viewing
Today 4:00 PM."

Hmm. Wonder what that is? Jesse thought to herself.

Chocolate Chips as Big as Soccer Balls

Chapter 6

The next morning started out fantastic. Jesse had a surreal dream about eating a humongous ice cream cone that was as big as a car and had chocolate chips as big as soccer balls—and Kimmy Kat Black with actual worms coming out of her actual ears.

Jesse's alarm clock woke her up at 6:00 am. The annoying DJ said, "This could be the hot, hot, hottest day this season, kiddos!"

Jesse hated it when the DJ said "kiddos." "I can't imagine it being any hotter than it was yesterday. Stubbs? Where are you?"

Jesse looked around. "Don't tell me," she said to herself. "In the sunbeam again, I'm willing to bet. Stubbs?" she called out again.

Yep. She was right. There he was. Stretched just as he was the morning before. Same spot. Same position. Toes up.

Jesse headed downstairs for breakfast. "C'mon, Stubbs," she called out to her cat, who was still asleep in the sunbeam. "You must be hungry too."

Jesse got some ice and poured herself a glass of juice. Looking up, she noticed the flower pot that was on the windowsill.

"What in the world happened here?" she asked herself. It seemed that the daisies that were fresh and perky just yesterday were all drooped over and appeared practically lifeless.

"I watered you guys just last night," she said. "What's up? You must be extra thirsty."

After Jesse took a few minutes to put more fresh water in the daisies' planter, she turned back to her juice glass.

"What?" she wondered out loud. "Now this?" The ice cube trays that she had set out just five minutes ago were melting all over the place.

"If it's not one thing, it's something else," she said to herself as she grabbed a sponge and began soaking up the mess.

Jesse finished her breakfast and called out to Stubbs again. "Dude. Let's go. Whaddaya say we head back upstairs and straighten up a bit more before we head out to the park?"

Jesse and Stubbs climbed the stairs to her room and, after making her bed, began to organize her messenger bag for the day. She set out the normal stuff as usual.

"Journal. Check. Pen and pencil. Check." She packed a few other things. "I think I'll bring my pocket calculator today," she said to Stubbs. "You never know when ya might have to calculate something."

Jesse reached for her magnifying glass in its holder on the windowsill. "I just might need my spyglass this time," she said as she placed it into her bag.

"WHAT IN THE WORLD!?" Jesse exclaimed at the sight before her eyes.

A Mystery? Unfolds?

Chapter 7

Jesse's eyes widened as she gazed upon the uncanny sight before her.

Her favorite crayon was on the windowsill, and it was mysteriously drooping. Bent entirely in half.

Jesse grabbed the crayon and held it up. "What in the world is going on here?" Jesse said in a mysterious whisper. "This crayon wasn't like this yesterday. Or the day before. Or the day before that." She was puzzled.

"In fact, this crayon has been in this very same spot for months now, and it's always been fine." She glanced at Stubbs with a perplexed look.

"Did you have something to do with this, Stubbs?" she said to the cat in a low, stern voice. Stubbs let out an innocent little mew and crawled under the bed.

Jesse tried to straighten the crayon out, but it was just as stiff as the others that were still in their box in her desk. "Well," Jesse said to Mr. Stubbs, who was now peeking out from beneath the bed, "you can't say I don't love a good mystery." She winked.

Jesse placed the crayon right back on the exact same spot where she had first found it all bent over. She studied it closely.

Okay, let's think about this logically, Jesse thought. She scratched her head. "This crayon has been in this very same spot for months and months. In fact, the last time I moved it was when I used it to make a Valentine's Day card. That was, let's see..." Jesse counted out the months on her fingers.

"February, March, April, May, June. Five months! This crayon has been in this very same spot for five months without a single change. Now what could have happened just yesterday to change it?" she wondered.

Jesse placed her hand on the windowsill. It was warm for sure. Very warm, in fact.

"But not hot enough to melt a crayon, that's for certain," she said to Stubbs, who had already found a new sunbeam to doze off in.

"Yep," she went on. "It was hot yesterday, but not really any hotter than it was the day before. Or the day before that. Or the day before that. Come to think of it, it's been hot all summer, and the crayon's been just fine." She scratched her head. "What was different about yesterday?"

Jesse continued to ruminate on the situation. "I think this calls for a little controlled observation," she said to Stubbs. "I have a suspicion that the heat of the sun had *something* to do with bending this crayon, but I can't imagine how. I'm going to conduct a little experiment."

Jesse pulled five fresh crayons from the box in her desk drawer.

"This should prove to be an interesting little analysis," she said to Stubbs, who was still asleep in the sunbeam.

"Stubbs, are you with me there, buddy?" she said to the cat.

Stubbs was still flat on his back and asleep, but his little paws were going a thousand miles an hour. "You must be dreaming about chasing something!" She laughed.

Jesse lined all five crayons up on the windowsill as close to where the bent crayon had been as she could.

"Now," she said to the still-sleeping cat as if he were listening, "we'll just come back here later today, and I'm sure we'll find that the sun has bent all five of the crayons, just as it had done to the other one."

The Mystery is Magnified

Chapter 8

Later that day, in her room, Jesse's experiment had proven to be a total bust.

"The crayons are just as we left them." She sighed. "I just don't get it."

Jesse decided to go outside and hang upside down from the The Thinkin' Tree.

"I do most of my greatest thinking when I'm upside down," she often said.

"I think gravity pushes all of my best thoughts and ideas down into my brain when I'm inverted," she liked to say.

"Who do we have here?" Jesse heard a familiar voice as she dangled. "Oh, hi," she said to Professor Peach from next door.

"I know you all too well, Jesse Steam. What's on your mind?" he asked. "You only hang upside down when you're trying to sort out a puzzle or solve a mystery."

Jesse explained the mystery of the crooked crayon on the windowsill.

"Well, it's no coincidence that the crayon melted on the windowsill, or near the summer solstice," the Professor professed.

"Summer solstice?" Jesse asked.

"Yes," the Professor continued. "The summer solstice occurs when one of Earth's

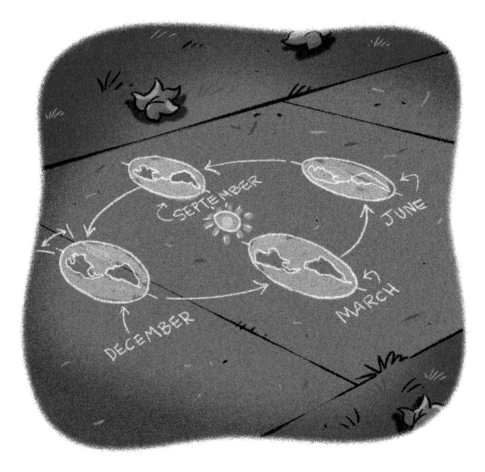

poles has its maximum tilt toward the Sun. It just so happens that yesterday the Sun was closer to us than on any other day of the year. *Only* 92.96 million miles (or 149.6 million kilometers) from Earth. That's a very short distance in celestial terms." The Professor drew a diagram of Earth's elliptical path around the Sun on the sidewalk with some chalk.

"Oh great," Jesse said. "Kimmy Kat Black was right. AGAIN! I'll never hear the end of this!" Jesse laughed.

"But that simple fact alone could not have melted the crayon," the Professor went on. "There must have been another mitigating factor associated with the alteration of your crayon," the Professor asserted. The Professor was always asserting something.

"Perhaps there was another object in play that helped to *magnify* the sun's intensity." He winked. "The glass pane in your window would have created a greenhouse effect, building more heat in your room, but certainly not enough to melt the crayon," he said.

Jesse thought hard. *What could have magnified the sun's intensity on the windowsill?* she asked herself silently.

"THAT'S IT!" Jesse shouted out loud. "My magnifying glass! I placed my spy glass in its stand on the windowsill yesterday for the first time in months!" she said with amazement. "That did it!"

"Jesse, my dear, it looks like you've solved the riddle of the crooked crayon on your own."

The Professor held Jesse's spy glass up and went on to explain. "You see, Jesse, the lens in your magnifying glass captured the sunlight and focused its intensity. The Sun produced the energy that fell on its convex lens in the form of light. Then the convex lens concentrated all of that light on to one small spot—like onto your crayon. This caused it to

heat up and melt right at the spot where the super-magnified sunbeam hit."

"Ya hear that, Stubbs? Another mystery solved," she said to the cat, who was sound asleep in another sunbeam.

THE END

Jesse's Word List

Annoying
like when your underwear is too tight

Berate
to scold—*Mom berated me when I burped at the table.*

Convex
having an outward curved surface—like your eyeball

Debacle
a failure—like when your test was a complete debacle

Deranged
confused—*I think my teacher is deranged.*

Elliptical
in the shape of an ellipse—you know, like an egg

Inverted
upside down—*I puke when I'm inverted.*

Peculiar
odd—*The school principal is very peculiar.*

Perplexed
baffled—*He was perplexed when I puked.*

Puke
to vomit—*I was inverted, so I puked.*

Repulsive
gross—*Giant, green boogers are repulsive.*

Ruminate
to think deeply about—*I ruminate about the word "ruminate."*

Sloppy
careless—*I don't care if I look sloppy when I'm playing in the mud.*

Snarky
being sharply critical—*My friend was snarky when I arrived covered in mud.*

Surreal
really, really weird or bizarre—*I had a surreal dream about riding a giant, three-headed kangaroo—in the mud.*

About the Author & Illustrator

Ken Bowser is an illustrator and writer whose work has appeared in hundreds of books and countless periodicals. While he's been drawing for as long as he could hold a pencil, all of his work today is created digitally on a computer. He works out of his home studio in Central Florida with his wife Laura and a big, lazy, orange cat.

Try It Out!

How to Make a Sundial Clock
Using the sun to tell the time is easier than you might think!

What You Need:
- A paper plate
- Some crayons or washable markers
- A sharpened pencil

Steps:

1. Decorate the back of the paper plate any way you like, or leave it blank.

2. Using your crayons or markers, draw a clock face on the plate as shown below.

3. With the help of an adult, carefully push the pointy end of the pencil through the very center of the plate. Now turn the pencil around and put the end with the eraser down through the plate.

4. Head outside and try out your awesome new sundial!

Note: Set your sundial on the ground in a sunny spot. Position the sundial with the "12" pointing north to determine the current time.

Check back with your clock throughout the day and watch the shadow move across the numbers on the plate indicating the time of day.

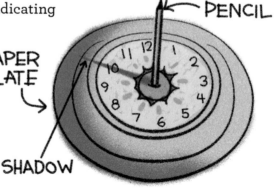

PENCIL

PAPER PLATE

SHADOW